Saving The Rhino In The Land Of Kachoo

Written by Tina Scotford

Illustrated by Frans Groenewald

JACANA

A poacher snuck into the land of Kachoo
Looking for rhinos - not one, but two!
He'd heard twin rhinos were recently born
And one of the twins had an extra large horn

He planned to swop the horn for cash
Material goods or expensive stash
He'd sell to the nation from over the ocean
That believed the horn held a magical potion

The poacher was small and his eyes were quite narrow
And packed on his back were his bow and his arrow
He crawled through the bushes on his hands and his knees
And slept in a cave in which he'd battled to squeeze

welcome to
KACHOO

By keeping well hidden and out of sight
He planned to sneak up on the rhinos at night
And once he saw them (through his eyes that were narrow)
He'd aim to shoot them with his bow and his arrow

The rhinos' good friend, the secretary bird
Was in charge of protecting the rhinoceros herd
He'd seen the man with his arrow and bow
And knew he was there to poach the rhino

The big five, the little five and an antelope herd
Were gathered together by the secretary bird

The bird flapped and spluttered
Then screamed out and stuttered:

"A poacher snuck into our land of Kachoo
Let's stop him now
It's what we must do!"

Elephant trumpeted then loudly said
"Find him for me
and I'll sit on his head!"

Leopard sprung forward
flashing her claw
"Leave him to me
and you won't see him no more!"

Buffalo bellowed
then said really quick
"I'll rid this man
with one powerful kick!"

Grawl! Roar!

The king of Kachoo
with the crown on his head
Stepped into the middle
and purred when he said

"I'll find this poacher as I've done so before
I'll frighten the man
with a growl and a roar!"

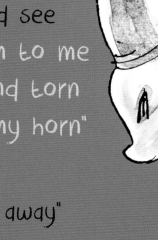

Rhino addressed the friends he could see
"Thanks for your offer but leave him to me
His bow and arrow will be ripped and torn
When I tear and shred them with my horn"

"Leave him to us, please, I say
We'll be the ones to chase him away"
Begged a tiny elephant shrew
One of the little five in the land of Kachoo

"That's kind of you, shrew, but dare I say
You're far too small to chase him away
I'm a rhino and will protect the crash"
Then off sped rhino in a lightning flash

The little five stood tall and remained undeterred
By what rhino had said and what they had heard
Then elephant shrew shared her marvellous plan
To once and for all rid Kachoo of this man

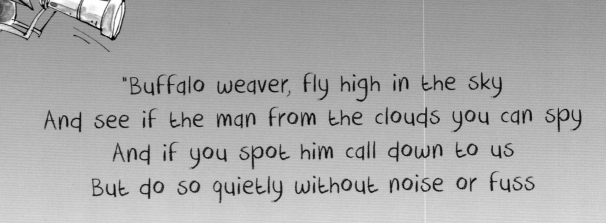

"Buffalo weaver, fly high in the sky
And see if the man from the clouds you can spy
And if you spot him call down to us
But do so quietly without noise or fuss

Leopard tortoise, your part is tricky
You need to move fast and find something sticky
The rest of us will distract the man
And foil his evil poaching plan"

The buffalo weaver, trusty old bird,
Found the man then kept to his word
The four friends went where the weaver said
To the cave that the man used at night for his bed

They found the poacher
with his bow and his arrow
Aiming at rhinos
through his eyes that were narrow

Quickly the shrew hopped high in the air
And knocked the long arrow way over there
The antlion burrowed out from the sand
Then flew to the man and bit him hard on his hand

Ready..
aim..

"Ouch!"
yelled the poacher
"What bit into me?
Who knocked my arrow
under that tree?"

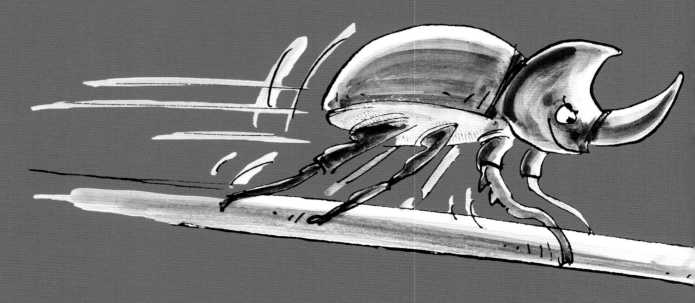

Again the man pulled on his arc-shaped bow
Aiming to shoot the large-horned rhino
But unbeknown to the silly man
The rhinoceros beetle was part of the plan

When the arrow was knocked by elephant shrew
The beetle knew then just what to do
His body was strong, stronger than iron
So when the man was bit by antlion
Beetle climbed onto the arrowhead tip
And clung on dearly for his airborne trip

The man pulled his bow
The arrow flew high
Gliding and sailing it soared through the sky

But it didn't land where the man had planned
Instead it bounced off
Not fast but slow
And fell from his target, the large-horned rhino

"How can that be?
I aimed perfectly
This time I won't miss!"
Said the man with a hiss

He spat out his gum
Then steadied his thumb
And pulled on his bow's flexible cord
High on the wind the arrowhead soared

It whizzed as it flew through the air so clear
Then, *pling*, it pierced the rhino's rear

PLING!

"I've got him now
He's mine, I say!"
Cheered the man
as he scrambled away
He waited and waited
for the rhino to fall
But still the rhino
stood steady and tall

The man shook his head
"What now?" he said
"Why hasn't he dropped?
Was the arrowhead stopped?"

Rhino turned round
and stuck to his bum
With the help of the poacher's
old chewing gum
Was the leopard tortoise
in his spotted shell
That had stopped the arrow
and split it as well

Suddenly appeared the rhino's dad
He was stomping and snorting and spitting mad
And together with him were his four famous friends
Growling and roaring:

"It's time poaching ends!"

The poacher ran frightened from the animals' sound
And off he sped, never again to be found

The rhino stood triumphant as the poacher fled
Then turned to his friends and softly said
"I can't thank you enough for what you have done
You saved a rhino. You saved my son

I wish we could teach the world out there
That our horns aren't magic; they're made from hair
They won't cure an illness or a disease
And they're not yours to take whenever you please"

The animals agreed with all that they'd heard
Then turned to listen to the secretary bird

"From this day forward I promise you
I'll find every poacher that enters Kachoo
And united we'll work as a victorious team
Chasing the poachers as they run off and scream"
The big five cheered with the brave little five
And together they chanted

"Keep our rhinos alive!"

First published by Jacana Media (Pty) Ltd in 2013

10 Orange Street
Sunnyside
Auckland Park 2092
South Africa
(+27 11) 628-3200
www.jacana.co.za

In collaboration with Neil Austen and 2sq Design (Pty) Ltd
© Text: Tina Scotford, 2013
© Illustrations: Frans Groenewald, 2013

ISBN 978-1-4314-0760-6

Editor: Dominique Herman
Designer: Jeannie Coetzee
Set in DK Crayon Crumble 22 pt
Job no. 001961
Printed by Tien Wah Press (Pte) Ltd

See a complete list of Jacana titles at www.jacana.co.za